The Very Boastful Kangaroo

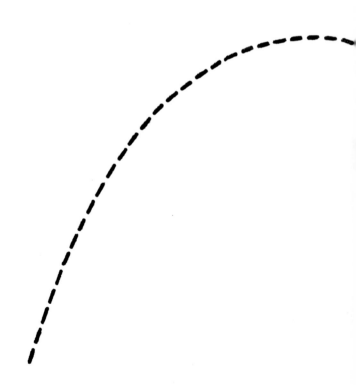

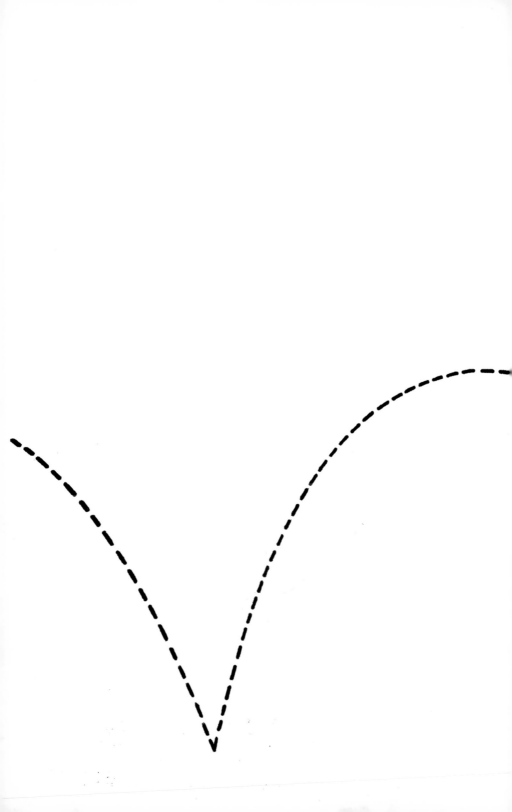

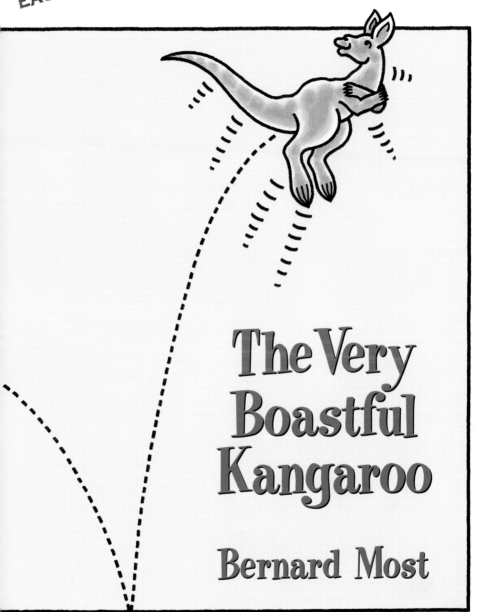

The Very Boastful Kangaroo

Bernard Most

Green Light Readers
Harcourt, Inc.

Orlando   Austin   New York   San Diego   Toronto   London

This story is about a very, very boastful kangaroo.
"I can jump so, so high!" he bragged.
"No one can jump higher than I can!"

Just then a little kangaroo jumped up. "Let's have a jumping contest," she said. "Can you jump higher than these kangaroos can?"

"Oh yes," said the very, very boastful kangaroo. "I can jump much, much higher than any kangaroo! I'll win the contest because I'm the best!"

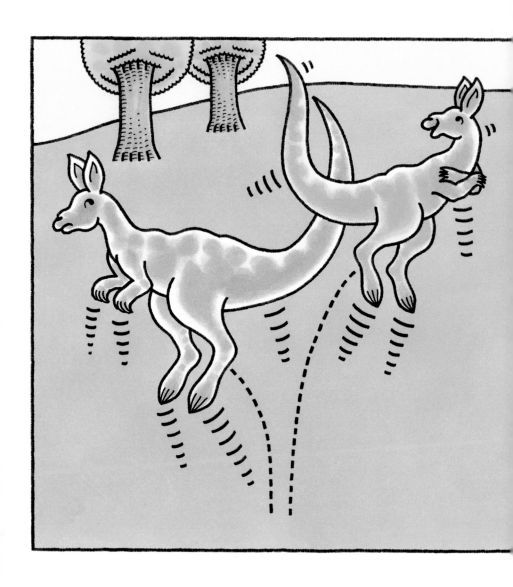

The first kangaroo jumped high.
The very, very boastful kangaroo
jumped even higher.

"See?" bragged the very, very boastful kangaroo. "I can jump higher. I'm the best!"

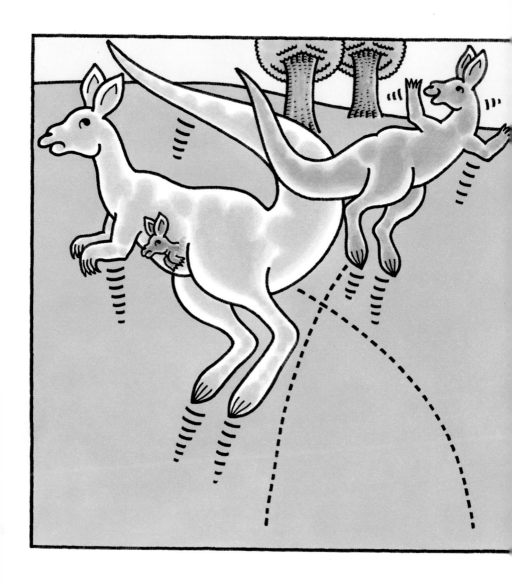

The next kangaroo jumped very high.
Even so, the very, very boastful
kangaroo jumped much higher.

"See?" the very, very boastful
kangaroo bragged. "I win! I win
the jumping contest."

"Not yet!" yelled a teeny, tiny kangaroo. "Can you jump higher than that tall tree?"

"That tree is much, much too tall!" said the very, very boastful kangaroo. "Even I can't jump higher than that tree!"

"If I jump higher than that tree, do I win the contest?" asked the teeny, tiny kangaroo.

The very, very boastful kangaroo
giggled. "Yes, but you're not going
to do it."

The teeny, tiny kangaroo jumped a
teeny, tiny jump. Then she shouted,
"I win! I win the contest…
BECAUSE TREES CAN'T JUMP!"

All the kangaroos giggled and
giggled—even the very, very boastful
kangaroo!

If You're Happy and You Know It

All the kangaroos were happy that the teeny, tiny kangaroo tricked the very, very boastful kangaroo. Join them in singing the song

"If You're Happy and You Know It."

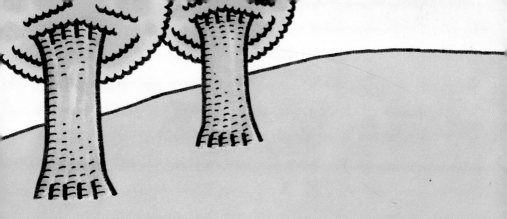

If you're happy and you know it,
clap your hands.

If you're happy and you know it,
clap your hands.

If you're happy and you know it,
then you'll really want to show it.

If you're happy and
you know it,
clap your hands.

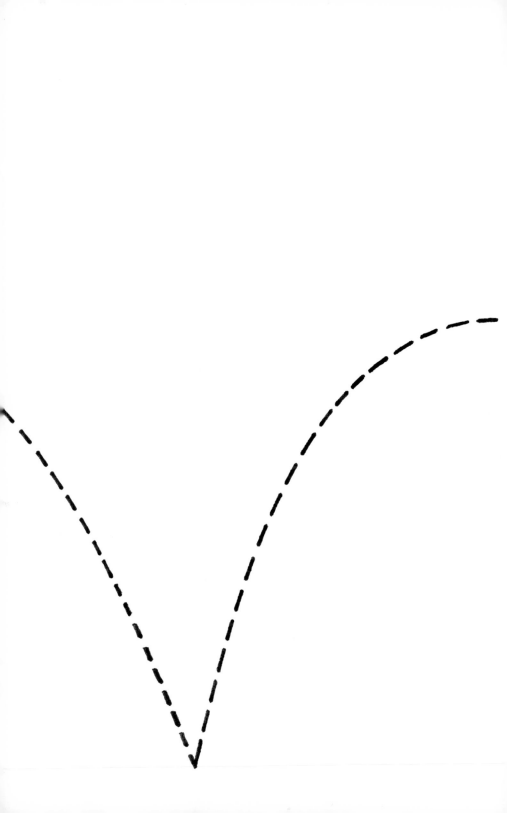

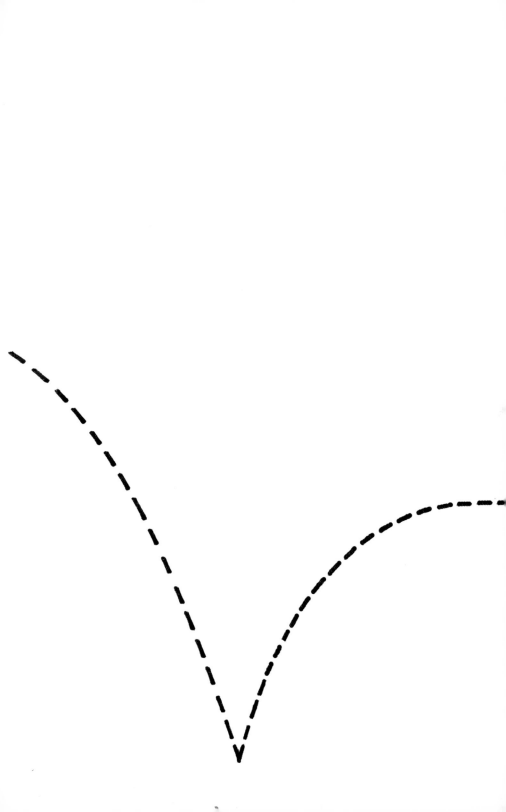

Meet the Author-Illustrator

Bernard Most likes his characters to find interesting ways to solve problems. In *The Very Boastful Kangaroo,* the teeny, tiny kangaroo finds a smart way to win the jumping contest. Bernard Most wants his readers to know that even though they are small, they can do anything they want if they just try. He always tells children to follow their dreams and to "never give up!"

Bernard Most

Requests for permission to make copies of any part of the work should be mailed to the following address: Permissions Department, Harcourt, Inc., 6277 Sea Harbor Drive, Orlando, Florida 32887-6777.

www.HarcourtBooks.com

First Green Light Readers edition 1999
Green Light Readers is a trademark of Harcourt, Inc., registered in the United States of America and/or other jurisdictions.

The Library of Congress has cataloged an earlier edition as follows:
Most, Bernard.
The very boastful kangaroo/Bernard Most.
p. cm.
"Green Light Readers."
Summary: A very, very boastful kangaroo brags that it can jump higher than anyone, but a teeny, tiny kangaroo cleverly wins the jumping contest.
[1. Kangaroos—Fiction. 2. Contests—Fiction.]
I. Title. II. Series.
PZ7.M8544Ve 1999
[E]—dc21   98-55234
ISBN 0-15-204880-4
ISBN 0-15-204840-5 (pb)

A C E G H F D B
A C E G H F D B (pb)

Ages 5–7
Grade: 2
Guided Reading Level: J–K
Reading Recovery Level: 18

Green Light Readers
For the reader who's ready to GO!

"A must-have for any family with a beginning reader."—*Boston Sunday Herald*

"You can't go wrong with adding several copies of these terrific books to your beginning-to-read collection."—*School Library Journal*

"A winner for the beginner."—*Booklist*

Five Tips to Help Your Child Become a Great Reader

1. Get involved. Reading aloud to and with your child is just as important as encouraging your child to read independently.

2. Be curious. Ask questions about what your child is reading.

3. Make reading fun. Allow your child to pick books on subjects that interest her or him.

4. Words are everywhere—not just in books. Practice reading signs, packages, and cereal boxes with your child.

5. Set a good example. Make sure your child sees YOU reading.

Why Green Light Readers Is the Best Series for Your New Reader

● Created exclusively for beginning readers by some of the biggest and brightest names in children's books

● Reinforces the reading skills your child is learning in school

● Encourages children to read—and finish—books by themselves

● Offers extra enrichment through fun, age-appropriate activities unique to each story

● Incorporates characteristics of the Reading Recovery program used by educators

● Developed with Harcourt School Publishers and credentialed educational consultants

Look for more Green Light Readers wherever books are sold!